P9-DGW-092

There Was a BOLD LADY Who Wanted a Star

by Charise Mericle Harper

First Edition

Library of Congress Cataloging-in-Publication Data

Harper, Charise Mericle.
There was a bold lady who wanted a star / by Charise Mericle Harper.—1st ed.
p. cm.
"Megan Tingley books."
Summary: In this variation on the traditional cumulative rhyme, a feisty woman tries roller skates, a bicycle, and even a rocket to reach a star.
ISBN 0-316-14673-0
1. Folk songs, English—England—Texts. [1. Folk songs—England. 2. Nonsense verses.] I. Title.
PZ8.3.H2185 Th 2002
782.42162'21—dc21
[E] 2001038114

10 9 8 7 6 5 4 3 2 1

MON-SP

Printed in Spain

The illustrations for this book were done in acrylic paint on chipboard, with collage elements. The text was set in Aunt Mildred, and the display types are Kruede and Hairspray Redhead.

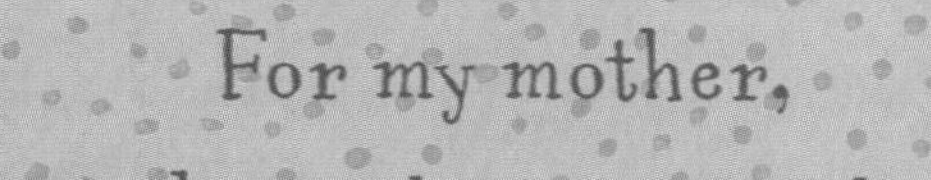

For my mother,
who has always been a very bold lady

There was a bold lady
who wanted a star.

N

I don't know why she wanted a star—

it seemed too far.

There was a bold lady who bought some shoes.

She ran for miles . . .

and then stopped for a snooze.

She bought the shoes to catch the star.
I don't know why she wanted a star—
it seemed too far.
SPACE BIRD
EARTH BIRD

There was a bold lady who bought some skates.

She slid and she slipped down hills . . .

and through gates.

She bought the skates
to replace the shoes.
She bought the shoes
to catch the star.

I don't know why she wanted a star—
it seemed too far.

There was a bold lady
who bought a bike.

What's not to like about riding a bike?

HONEY

She bought the bike

to replace the skates.

She bought the skates

to replace the shoes.

She bought the shoes

to catch the star.

I don't know why

she wanted a star—

it seemed too far.

There was a bold lady
who bought a car.

BE
FRIENDLY • COURT
OBEDIENT • CHEERF
EAT MORE CAKE
TASTY
YUMMY
6TH FLOOR
CAKES
PIZZA
SUNSHINE HATS
SHOE REPAIR
SOCK WORLD
CLOSED
BIG CITY DELI
HONEY-BEE
NEWS-PAPERS FOR SALE

She drove for a while but she couldn't go far.

She bought the car
to replace the bike.
She bought the bike
to replace the skates.

She bought the skates
to replace the shoes.

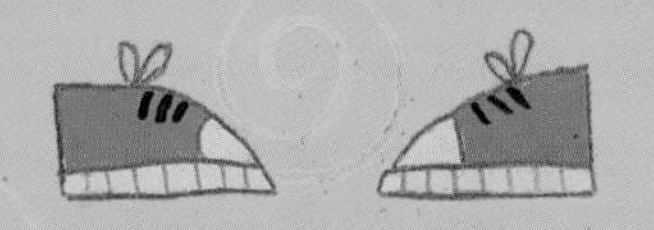

She bought the shoes
to catch the star.
I don't know why she wanted a star—
it seemed too far.

There was a bold lady
who bought a plane.

She flew through snow and she flew through rain.

SPEEDY

She bought the plane to replace the car.

She bought the car to replace the bike.

She bought the bike to replace the skates.

She bought the skates to replace the shoes.

She bought the shoes to catch the star.

I don't know why she wanted a star—

it seemed too far.

There was a bold lady
who bought a big rocket,

then zoomed up and caught the star in her pocket.

She rode the rocket
back to the plane.

She flew the plane
back to the car.

She skated on skates
back to the shoes.

She drove the car
back to the bike.

She pedaled the bike
back to the skates.

She ran for miles and
didn't stop for a snooze.

There was a bold lady who wanted a star.
Now I know why she wanted the star . . .
to put in a jar. (So it wasn't so far!)

LUCY ROBBINS WELLES LIBRARY
3 2510 09590 1534